Written by James Allen & Amy Holman
Illustrated by Kah Yan Choong

For our favourite huggers, Holly, Gaius and Speckie.

First published in Great Britain in 2022 by Pterodactyl Publishers Ltd

Storyboard designed by Kah Yan Choong and Joe N. Brown

ISBN: 978-1-7397255-1-8

A CIP catalogue record for this book is available from the British Library.

Hugasaurus

James Allen & Amy Holman

Illustrated by
Kah Yan Choong

Once upon a long, **long** time ago

there lived a Hugasaurus and
although he had little, tiny arms,

he absolutely loved...

He hugged his toys.

He hugged his plants.

Not the **spiky** ones though.

And his all time favourite things to hug were

But he was a T. rex and they had a teeny bit of a reputation for being...

absolutely **terrifying.**

It was a problem.

"What you need" said Dadasaurus,
"is a dinosaur that isn't scared to hug you."

"Like you?" asked Hugasaurus.
"No, not me," said Dadasaurus.

"I can't hug both you **and** Mumasaurus all the time..."

The next day Hugasaurus set off,
to find a dinosaur that wasn't afraid of him.

First he saw Miss Fabulosaurus and held out his arms for a hug.
But she thought he was **chasing** her and ran away.
"Stay back!" she shrieked, "you'll smudge my makeup."

Then he spotted Sickasaurus and gave a big smile.

But Sickasaurus got **scared** by those long, pointy teeth and she ran away.

“I’m infectious!” she yelled, “don’t come any closer.”

Next, he found Partysaurus,
so asked if he'd like a hug.

But Partysaurus thought it
was a **trick** and he ran away.

"I'm late for a party!" he yelped,
with his tail between his legs.

"This is hopeless," sighed Hugasaurus,
clutching a nearby rock.

"I'm **never** going to get a hug."

The **rock** hugged him.

Which was surprising, to say the least.

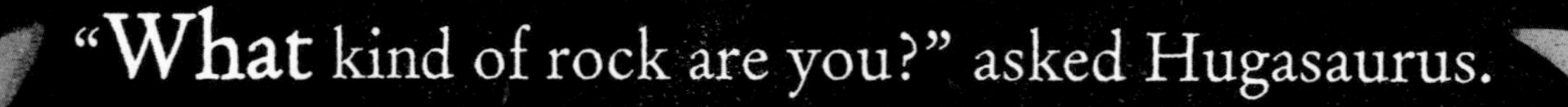

"**What** kind of rock are you?" asked Hugasaurus.

"I'm, err, umm, Hugarock!" it said.

Hugasaurus looked puzzled,
"I've never met a
Hugarock before."

"Well, I'm quite unique and certainly **no** good to eat, because I'm a rock, so I'd break your teeth."

"But I do **love** hugs.
You can hug me all you want,"
said Hugarock matter-of-factly.

"I'd like that," said Hugasaurus, so he took Hugarock home.

He **loved** hugging Hugarock... for it was unusually warm.

And soft, not like any other rock he knew.

And it was just the right size for his little arms.

And it always seemed to be right next to him,
even when he left it elsewhere.

Another funny thing about Hugarock, ever since it had moved in, there were little rock piles all over the place.

They did **not** smell good.

Also, food had been disappearing and well...

it was **very** talkative, for a rock.

"Call me a **Suspiciousaurus**," said Hugasaurus rubbing his chin, "but I'm starting to suspect it might not be a rock at all."

That night, Hugasaurus set a

CANNED BREAD

He was woken suddenly from
his sleep, by a **crash** of cans.

He **jumped** out of bed,

leapt down the stairs

Clang!!

Clink!!

and **guess** what
he found?

Hugarock!!

"You're no rock," said Hugasaurus. **"You tricked me!"**

"No, I'm not a rock," squeaked Hugarock. "I'm a pangolin and I didn't want to trick you, but I thought you were going to eat me."

"I do really love hugs."

"Maybe I should **eat** you?"
roared Hugasaurus.

Hugarock suddenly looked very scared,
which made Hugasaurus feel bad.

He didn't really want to gobble him up;
he was just cross about being tricked.

“I have an idea,” said Hugasaurus.
“Instead of me eating you, maybe we could be friends?”

“I’d like that,” said Hugarock.

So Hugasaurus let him out of the trap.

"**Sorry** for saying I was a rock,"
said Hugarock.

"**Sorry** for saying I would
eat you," said Hugasaurus.

And then the two of them made up properly,
with a great, big...

hug.

The end